Sandy Creek
122 Fifth Avenue
New York, N.Y. 10011

ISBN - 13: 978 - 1 - 4351 - 1158 - 5

Printed and bound in China

1 3 5 7 9 10 8 6 4 2

 *from an idea by* ANDREA DAMI

Illustrations by Marco Campanella
Text by Anna Casalis
Design by Stefania Pavin

TIP THE MOUSE

DOESN'T WANT TO GO TO NURSERY SCHOOL

Illustrated by

Marco Campanella

SANDY CREEK

Today is Tip's first day of nursery school. But Tip is very unhappy!

"I don't want to go!" he says loudly, digging in his heels. "Teddy doesn't want to go either! We want to stay at home with you, Mom!"

Tip argues so much that he finally gets his way. His mom (chuckling to herself) says, "Okay, Tip! Today you can stay at home with me and keep me company while I do some housework!"

She starts ironing. Tip watches her, happy that he doesn't have to go to nursery school.

Next, his mother mops the floor.
"I hope that she will finish soon!" thinks Tip. "It isn't much fun to just sit here looking at her! I can't wait until she can play with me a bit!"
But Mom doesn't have time to play with him – she's too busy!

HUMPH!

Mom has finally finished the cleaning. But …

RING! RING! The phone rings. It's Aunt Nelly, with lots of news.

"Will they ever stop talking?" grumbles Tip, trying to get his mother's attention.

Finally Mom takes Tip out to do the shopping.

But when they get there she meets her best friend, and she simply has to tell her all the news Aunt Nelly has just told her. So they chat, and chat and chat …

"It's so boring!" complains Tip, who is tired of listening to them. "Hey look! What's that sign over there? I think I'll go and have a look!"

Tip peeks through the window of the nursery school. All his friends are there. "They seem to be having a lot of fun!"

That night, Tip asks, "Mommy, do you mind if I don't keep you company tomorrow? I was thinking that I would like to go to nursery school!"

His mom smiles. "Of course, darling! I'm happy that you've realized that it's more fun to go to nursery school than to stay at home all day!"

So the next morning Tip wakes up early and happily skips to nursery school with his mom. She stops for a moment to talk to the teacher while Tip's friends run to welcome him.

"Hi, Tip!" they all shout.

On the slide, Tip hugs Teddy and goes down. "**YIPPEE!** Look how fast I am!" He is already having a lot of fun.

At nursery school, there are so many toys! They are different from the ones he has at home. And best of all, he has lots of friends to play with!

After playing all morning, Tip eats his lunch. Afterwards, he starts to feel sleepy.

The teacher shows him the special Nap Room where kids can sleep.

"Have a nice nap!" says the teacher. But Tip is already sound asleep.

When they wake up, all the little mice go back to their games.

"Is it time to go home, already?" wonders Tip when he sees his mom and dad arrive.

He is sorry that the day is already over, but he is happy to see his parents – he has so many wonderful things to tell them!

HELLO!

"It's so much fun!" he tells his dad, giving him a kiss. "We played, we drew pictures, we sang, we ate, we slept and then we played again. The teacher is really nice! I like her a lot. And do you want to know the best thing about it? Tomorrow I can go back again!"

NURSERY SCHOOL